Things I Should
Keep to Myself

JILL MARIE KELLY

NEWMAN SPRINGS PUBLISHING
320 Broad Street
Red Bank, NJ 07701

First originally published by Newman Springs Publishing 2018

ISBN 978-1-64096-628-4 (Paperback)
ISBN 978-1-64096-629-1 (Digital)

Printed in the United States of America

For Mom and Dad

Sight

The eye sees only what the mind
Is prepared to comprehend

Christopher's Story

So I've had some abilities since I was a girl. I usually see spirits and I can communicate with people in the twilight of life and death. Aunt Claudia came down from Maine, basically to say good-bye to her son, Christopher, who had been in the hospital since October. He was on limited time, had cancer that spread, and we didn't know how long he had. She arrived this past Tuesday, visited Chris every day. He was mostly unresponsive. She spent seven hours with him on Friday, he didn't move. His skin was stretched tight over his bones. I knew it was time to help.

Friday night, in the middle of my sleep, I heard Chris' deep voice saying he wanted to see me. I woke up and knew it would be a taxing day. I grabbed my labradorite stone pendant for clarity and comfort.

We went into the hospice, got some courage from coffee, and I walked into his room. His skin was stretched across his skeleton like an unwrapped mummy. His eyes were sunken into his head and half open. I knew he couldn't see well.

I grabbed his hand and said, "Chris, it's cousin Jill. I can hear you."

I put the labradorite pendant in his palm between our hands. He immediately squeezed my hand and moaned a bit. When the nurse came in she didn't believe me. I proceeded with my mom, Chris' godmother, and Aunt Claudia, his mother, for three hours communicating with him. Finding out his last wishes, his fears, and his last messages to loved ones. It was surreal. I could hear him as if he was sitting up and talking, but it was past that now. He couldn't sit up, he couldn't talk, but I heard every word he wanted to say. And there were many past loved ones I could see in the room waiting to comfort him. Grandma was there to take his hand into the realm of light, love, and happiness. She smiled at me.

Chris was scared. He "said" things, had thoughts in his mind that I could tap into. I could hear him.

"I'm scared, Jill, I don't want to be buried; I don't want to be in the dark and be worm food."

I comforted him from the knowledge I had gained from spirits who have crossed.

"Chris," I said, "There is a rope of love above us and our job as earth-dwellers is to take our thread from the rope and weave it, learn how to love unconditionally, and when we die our love gets woven into the rope once more. It's a bit profound and a lovely way of looking at life and death. They told me you are met when you die with the light of the loved ones that have crossed, those that you positively impacted in life. They told me you have a choice after you die to become a guardian of those on earth or to move on and let your energy be recycled, however that works, I don't know. But I know energy has neither been created nor destroyed since the beginning of time, so it obviously gets recycled somehow."

My aunt looked at my mom. "She can really hear him?"

"Yes," my mother replied and looked at me to go on.

Chris took in what I told him for a bit, and I heard him say, "I'm scared; will I get judged?"

Chris had been out of our lives for sixteen years and he was nervous that his addiction and his decision to keep us out of his life for so long was going to get him in the end.

And I said, "No, from what I've learned in my relationship with spirits, you see your life, you review it, and you join the love, you are healthy and free of pain. Most spirits don't want to be recycled, they want to stay in the realm of happiness and light forever. Grandma is here and Grandpa Ben, and a cat."

I started laughing, it's rare that I see animals.

I held his hand and kissed him, "Chris, you don't need to be scared and we will all be relieved when you exit your shell of pain and suffering. We will be here and we love you and that has never stopped and never will."

He moaned and mouthed the word "Mom" and reached his hand out for Aunt Claudia. She was astonished, he hadn't moved for days.

He said, "I'm afraid since I was out of your lives for sixteen years that you stopped loving me."

I said, "That is impossible, love doesn't stop and you can be a guardian to your new niece and nephew and we will still feel your love. Protect them."

He moaned and squeezed my hand and liked that idea.

He was worried, "Will I only be with one family member at a time?"

I said, "The cool thing about spirits is that they are omnipresent and can be with everyone all the time."

We called my sister, Laura, who couldn't be there with us and she said on speakerphone, "Chris, there are a lot more people waiting for you than those who need to say good-bye."

He was still scared and I kept kissing his hand.

I said, "You will love where you are about to go, with no pain and all the food you want."

He said, "That's good, I haven't eaten in a while."

At one point, a strong smell of flowers came to me, Aunt Claudia, and mom. It was a mixture of scents like a bouquet, not a specific smell. It lasted about two minutes. We looked it up when we left, apparently when a body is close to death it emits an odor because of chemicals being released from a body that has been starving. (The religious explanation says saints like Saint Teresa of the Roses, the rose smell came and lingered for days after she died—meaning that her body was holy and full of grace.)

Chris and I "talked" more and we learned where he wanted his ashes scattered.

Chris explained, "My sign to you will be music. Meaning when you think of me if the radio or TV plays a song, it's me saying hello."

We happened to have a radio channel on the TV, in his room, as we sat there. "This Time" by Troy Shondell came on the music station on the TV.

I said, "Mom, Aunt Claudia, this is what he means, listen to the words."

The song played…

This time we're really breaking up
This time we said way too much
This times for all time
How about this time
This time there'll be no goodnight kiss
This time is forever
This time I find that I'm
Really losing you

My heart is broken no
It really doesn't matter anyhow
Now that you're going away
I only live from day to day
This time there'll be no goodnight kiss
This time is forever
This time I find that I'm really losing you.

Mom looked at me and looked at Aunt Claudia, and we were all crying. Music really communicates.

Dad, who was in the waiting room this whole time, came in and just checked on us. I was still holding Chris' hand and tears streamed down my face.

"Jill's doing her voodoo shit," he said with a smile.

Chris said, "I always had respect for your father."

I said, "Well, he was the one who convinced you to sign the damn papers to come here."

My dad had sat with him and explained that he required more care than anyone could give him at home and that he really was not going to get better, although he was forty-six years old. So when Chris was still of sound mind he signed the papers to go to hospice. That was two weeks ago. As soon as dad walked out of the room, the music station on the TV played "Sitting on the Dock of the Bay" by Otis Redding. That happens to be my father's favorite song. We knew that was a sign.

Many things were said. He told me where in Maine he wanted his ashes scattered. And how we all had to be there to do it. And to take a stone from the beach when we do.

He said, "I'm sorry for not being the best son and big brother. I want to say thank you to you Aunt Dianne, Uncle Bill, Cousin Laura, and Jim."

Jim was his best friend who came to see him almost every day for two months and finally decided to reach out to us to reunite Chris and his family.

He thanked Aunt Claudia and said, "You still love me, right, mom?"

Aunt Claudia said in staggered speech through her tears, "How could I ever stop loving you, you're my son."

Chris said, "I'm okay now, it's alright for you all to go."

"Are you sure, Chris? Cause we can stay as long as you need."

I looked down at my watch, three hours had passed that seemed like ten minutes. I knew I would be drained when we left. The music on the TV changed and we heard,

I'll be alone each and every night
While you're away, don't forget to write
Bye bye, so long, farewell
Bye bye, so long...

We all looked at each other again and cried.

I looked at him and said, "Chris, that was not nice!"

And we laughed through our tears. The song was "See you in September." We kissed him good-bye, my mom leaned in and said "I love you. You remember that red heart necklace you gave me when you were ten? I have it and I'll wear it and think of you."

Aunt Claudia got close to his ear and said, "I will always love you." And she kissed his forehead.

I said, "I'll still talk to you, okay? and you can visit me any time." As I walked out I heard his faint voice say, "Midnight, good-bye."

We came home and had a good night, ate mom's goulash, talked, cried, and laughed. We told stories of the past, family, and pain, and the joy of being together again.

I went upstairs to go to sleep. I lit a black candle on my night stand to give light to Chris's darkness. I said a prayer, "When the light goes out, Chris, let go." The candle extinguished at 12:10 a.m. The smell of smoke filled the room and the phone rang. He was gone.

Thank you, Chris, for bringing us all together again. Thank you for your life though it may not have been the one you would have chosen. Rest now, my friend, we will always love you.

Valentine

You matter

You are loved

You have touched a life in a way that you may never know

There is a person out there that remembers the times you have both shared, and those times may not be the times that you specifically remember, but they have happened, and the memories are cherished

There is someone who thinks of you when you are not thinking of them

That wonders how you are

That hopes that you are okay

That wishes you all the best in everything you do

There is a person out there that never forgot a kind word you may have said

There is a person out there that will always listen when you need a friend

There is a person out there that thinks of you when a specific song is heard

And laughs, and maybe even cries

There is a person that misses you and lives for the time they can see you again

There is a person that has a memory of you when you were little,

When you were at your worst,

When you were at your best

There is a person that has maybe only known you a few weeks,

A few months,

A few years,

And by just being you
You have made a difference in their lives
There is a person,
And if you can't think of them,
Then think of me
For you are one or all of these things and more
Celebrate this day, not just for your wife, husband, boyfriend, girl-
friend, but for everyone in your life that has shared with you
love, however fleeting it may have been, for love leaves warmth
in our hearts and fingerprints on our souls.

A Sunrise and a Fawn

The lifeless fawn
Neck twisted and distorted
Beside the soft gentle fur of its body
Small drops of blood splattered on its coat
Like tears streaming from its once pain-filled eyes
On the side of the rush hour traffic
Against the purple and pink clouds of dawn
Death is mixed with life
A sunrise and a fawn

Size of New York

So much fashion
with homeless veterans outside churches
with the hungry right there
The end of summer
Hot
Worrying what to wear
Beauty and pain walking by
People watching
while you do your morning routine
Pushing a stroller
Conversations with a six-year-old about compliments
and acts of kindness
So many shapes and sizes
Twenty-five walk by in a matter of seconds
You sometimes stand in a group of thirty just to cross the street
Unpleasant smells in the August wind
And it's real
In your face
Homeless veterans
Women begging, pregnant with no shoes
you appreciate the life in everything
A fun outfit
A gorgeous hat
A suit so crisp it makes you smile
An old woman with crazy orange sunglasses with wings
The shoe shiners that wink as you walk by
The tourists stopping in mid-stride for a perfect picture
of something that's ordinary to you

But the first time you stop to and look at what they see
The freshness of something new
At first you are in awe that people wear,
Act,
and do certain things you judge
She's too big for that
That jacket's not right on him
Wow that dress is like a handkerchief
And after a few weeks
and looking at everything people are people
The lowest juxtaposed against the richest there are
That's New York
You start seeing confidence
People comfortable in their skin
No shame
Just happy
And yes some try very hard for attention
And shock value
But they are one of many
You see the ordinary in the extreme
And the reality in between
And we are all a part of a gigantic pulse
A heartbeat of differences
Which makes us so much the same

Preschool Teacher

I want to be an inspiration
The reason they want to come to school
Be the story they tell at night
The reason they follow the rules
Help them be courageous
Help their confidence when they speak up
Help them sing their song
Hold them when they tear up
Sing them to sleep
Tuck them in
Tell them I love them very much
Chase their fears and worries away
Wipe their tears with a gentle touch
I am so much to them
The constant that they've known
And I'll have to say good-bye one day
And they may forget me when they're grown
But please know I loved every single one of them
as if they were my own

Loving a poet is your
Key to immortality

All She Wanted

All she wanted was time to
Share with you
A blushing smile
The touch of your hand
On hers
Shared time
Expensive time
Priceless moments
To cherish

Stains

She draws you in
Her petals of pink softness
Her scent
Dizzying wild whiffs
Surround you
You reach to pluck her
From her loneliness
Her solitary pain
Thorns of blood
Dare to stain
Your smile
And you love her still

Rainbow of Emotion

She was
Crimson with passion
Blue with shame
Green with jealousy
Of a different name
Violet with hope
Trying to cope
The whole rainbow of emotion
Ignoring the notion
That everything will be okay
And she loved anyway

Sometimes you need to hold on to those who care
With both hands

Little Girl

Take care of her
The way mothers do
The little girl inside of you
Watch out for danger
Look both ways
Beware of strangers
On lonely days
Keep her safe way down deep
And honor all
The promises
You keep
Next time you make a choice
Listen to her tiny voice
Remember her image
Remember her smile
Remember you would never
Harm this child
For she is a part of you
In everything you do
Take care of her
The way mothers do

Finding a Way

"You want the crazy truth?
My thoughts are like children on fire running off a roof"

The doctor said, "Let me explain
It's like she's high on every drug and she feels no pain"
When she crossed traffic and did not look left or right
Heard a small sound and then turned in fright
Met the grill of an eighteen-wheeler
Met it eye to eye
The truck driver jumped out and tried to stop her cry
She looked up at his haggard face and asked him, "Where am I?"
He said, "You're safe now, please don't start to cry."
Next thing she knew she was in the hospital room
Remembered an ambulance and sirens but it happened so soon
She told the nurse, "I'm only drinking water and haven't gotten any
    sleep."
The nurse asked, "For how long?"
She smiled, "For about a week."
Meanwhile her boyfriend, friend, and mom had no idea where she
    was
Missing for two days wondering around in pajamas like she does
The nurse said, "We have to see if you're with child
or I won't be able to calm you down for a while."
Jill picked up the phone and called her love

She said, "Our prayers have been answered, this is what dreams are
    made of...
They think I might be pregnant, are you home?"
He said,
"Jill, please put the nearest person on the phone."

He and her family had been calling hospitals and police officers for
    the past two days
Thinking I was killed or raped or in a the ditch and thrown away
The only way I know how to describe that time
even though I was in my own head
I had no control of my mind
And my loved ones thought I was dead
they locked me away for a couple weeks
Diagnosed me with everything after spinal tap shrieks
After the drugs I don't remember a full year
In deep depression I don't remember my twenty-first birthday or my
    first legal beer

So thank you Mr. Truck Driver that the hospital has no record of
you saved my life that day
My mind holds a snapshot of you
Sweeping me up off the highway

I'm so happy your brakes worked and that your truck didn't hit the
    frail thing that I was

You gave me my second chance
I won't waste it
Like everyone else does
I'll teach with love
Take care of the world

I'm stronger now
No longer that girl
Barefoot and wet
With flowers in her hair
That crazy one
…She's in there somewhere

Every time I look at the sky
Hear the honk of an eighteen-wheeler go by
I remember your words
"You're safe now, please don't start to cry."
You see, sir,
You passed your angel wings to me that day
And now after seventeen years
I'm ready to find my way

Laying

Laying in the arms
of someone that understands
Feeling deep inside
The desire in his hands
Love
An emotion played with
But know
The longer you linger
The further you'll go

What You See

It kills me that you see yourself
Filled with so much hate
One day you'll be okay
And till that day
I'll wait
One day I hope you look back and realize
Why so much of this is wrong
For I refuse for you to become in my heart
Just a memory in a song

She Is

She's an angel
A gentle tiger
A mermaid
A moon child
Who flies on the wings
Of ravens
Glows in the darkness
And swims in her pain
She's magic
She's madness
She's comfort
And passion
In the wisp of a flame
That jumps at the sound
Of her name

Mood green eyes
That try to subdue
The pieces of pain
Inside of you

Our Kind of Miserable

My soldier
Stroking my hair as I listen to his heartbeat
I don't care how he holds me
As long as we are so close
I can feel him breathe
I crave it
And we are both far from perfect
And the future is scary
And I don't know what will be
But if we do it together
While he holds onto me
And keeps me close
I can deal with our kind of miserable
The kind that feels like you need to start over
In the middle of life
But the love is overflowing
And your heart is happy
And you feel safe and protected in your lover's arms
And you run away from life just to kiss him in moonlight
Not bad
Our kind of miserable

Still

We all want love
Need to love
Crave love
And look around
To see whom we can tack it on
But we don't need anyone
To understand where love comes from
For it is always within you
The power that drives you
Share it with whomever you will
But inside is where it lies
If you are still

Intoxication

I'm having visions of you
In the flickering twilight of
The massive candle
The bitter perfume of the past
Remains on my skin
Wash me with the holy water of your tongue
Touch me with your blessed hand
I wanna feel something I can believe in
Your own sacred religion
Preach with kisses
Build up the physical miracle
Be the prophet of my future
Cross me with your eyes
Drink from my mouth
Eat from my lips
Breathe with my air
Stay forever.

The Kissing Spell

Kissing in the rain
Kiss away the past
Kiss away the fear
The kissing spell is cast
Do nothing
Feel my love
Say you want me
It just grows
Say you'll be there
Rise above
Lord I need you heaven knows
My dark angel
Wrap your wings
Around all my broken things
Mend the hurt with your eyes
Hold my hand and hypnotize
I want to hold you until I sleep
I want to love you 'til I weep
So you can see yourself how true
My love really is for you

Those eyes
Deep seas of blue and pain
Of love and strain
Constellations of timelessness
Trapped in the irises
And I am his

Daydream

And I will daydream of
that moment
That fell like
Gentle rain
Windswept and breathless
When you kissed me

Made Of

A storm is made of flakes
An ocean is made of drops
My heart is made of memories

Prayer

A light in the dark
A flame
A prayer on the whisper of a child
she picks up the stick and finds a candle to light her own
How young does she have to be to teach her that there's
something bigger
Something
that loves her unconditionally
to have faith in what she can't see
so she says her prayers silently
like a birthday wish as she lights her
flame
And maybe it is
A penny in a fountain
A wish on the first star
but it means something
at this moment it means
Everything
to her
and to me

It Wasn't Me

I have walked arm in arm with the spirits of the dead. They have taken me to past lives to share their experiences with me. They have come to me when they felt confused, seeing through my eyes the reality of the present.

I sat in deep concentration in the aftermath of my parents' cocktail party. I had already finished two glasses of wine and a screwdriver. I tried to sit still and watch television. I tried not to talk. I did my best to act sober. I lost all attempted focus when she tapped on the window. I saw her out of my peripheral vision. She tapped again and drew me in to look at her. Sweat and a tear dripped down her ethereal face. Her hair, like threads of golden yarn, was wet and clung to her neck to avoid the wind. Her ice blue eyes burned through me. She tapped again with the delicate tips of her nails. Her face shone through the massive glass window. I tried to resist looking back. I tried to overcome the curiosity slowly rising within me. "*She's not there*," I kept repeating in my head. She tapped again. Her eyebrows narrowed in anger of being ignored. She grew desperate. She knew no one else could see her but me. She knew I was the only one that might be able to help her. She needed my eyes. I gave in. Everything went black.

My boyfriend decided to take me to the guest bedroom, the closest place to lay down. He was nervous and didn't know what to expect. I was having dizzy spells. He stood me up and helped me walk from the family room to the kitchen. Every now and again I would faint, forcing him to carry my deadweight until I recovered. My nylons impaired me from walking without slipping on the polished kitchen tile. Considering I was intoxicated, balance was a difficulty.

When we finally reached the room, he placed me on the bed. I lay there with a tight, backless, floor-length, velvet dress on, upset and distressed, in a position that mimicked a chalk outline of a murder scene. She was with me. I could feel her. Goose bumps covered my body. I could tell that she was frightened. He held me, not knowing what was going on inside my head, not knowing what I could see, even though my eyes were closed. I could see her. She entered me slowly, taking control of every sense, every muscle. She started using my eyes to search for an answer, an answer to why she still roamed the earth. I was shaking, crying, and sobbing. But it wasn't me. Streams of black tears ran from the corners of my eyes like veins across my face. My lips trembled. It wasn't me.

My sister came into the room. She witnessed him dragging me across the house to the room and wanted to know what was happening to me. They talked in what I perceived as only muffled tones, almost another language. I couldn't move. I couldn't say anything. I wanted to scream. I wanted to get her out of me. I was paralyzed. My sister looked into my eyes, but it wasn't me. Gasping in horror she turned to him.

"Really look into her eyes," he said with misunderstanding.

She did so. I looked back, but didn't recognize her. Like a child caught in a crowd of strangers, madly searching for her mother, I pushed her away, unable to realize that she was my sister.

"Jill, it's me!" she cried.

I blankly started at her. I wasn't her sister. My sister threw a glance at him.

"Why doesn't she know me? Why doesn't she—"

"It's not her. Something is inside of her," his focus turned to me. "It's okay," he held me close to him, rocking me with the same gentleness a mother would have toward her baby.

My sister stroked my hair.

"Sweety, it's me, Laura, I'm here," her voice was desperate and confused.

He looked directly into my eyes. "Oh my God! Look at her eyes!"

"What," she replied.

"They're blue."

"Yeah, so."

"Her eyes are green! Her eyes... are changing!"

I didn't know them. I was frustrated. I was caught in an unknown place, searching for something familiar, some kind of clue to tell me why I was there. It wasn't me. I woke up. My boyfriend and sister were hovering over me. My mother had just walked into the room. I looked at all of them. They immediately jumped back.

"What happened?" I screamed.

"Your eyes... they're green," he said in a whisper.

"They're always green," I said.

"But they were just blue," he mumbled.

Silence strangled them.

"It wasn't you," my sister said, awestruck.

I then realized what they were saying. I had been taken over again, by the spirit of a girl who burned in the house where my house now stands. My eyes being the window to an answer, she took them over, in return changing them, changing them to her own.

"*Why?* Why does this happen? Why to me?"

I was hysterical. I buried my face in my boyfriend's chest and cried. My voice shook with misunderstanding, anger, and despair. She was gone.

These Ordinary Hands

So many have been touched
With these hands
So many have felt their softness
Experienced their healing
Enjoyed their comfort
So many have felt them run
Over their eyelashes
Through their hair
Gentle, and sometimes hurtful
Some have wrapped their love
Their affection
Around these fingers
Some took back what they gave
Leaving them naked and pale
Some admired them from afar
And wished for one loving touch
Some let go of them too quickly
These hands didn't just touch the surface
Of your skin
These hands held you from within

A Memory

A hug
A brush against my skin
A whisper in my ear
A comfort
A moment
A memory

Storm

The thunder
Serenades me
The lightning casts ominous shadows
So quickly
Goodnight, Mother Moon
Your drops of love
Will lull me to sleep

Gaze

We look up when we wonder
To the skies our eyes gaze
We can't extinguish
Our hope in the sun's forgiving rays
The moon beams bright
At the end of the days
Stars twinkle
Every night
Sometimes soar away
Some wish
Some pray
That a little answer
Will find its way and stay

Watching spring rain
Under the full moon
Dreaming of summer
My heart's in full swoon

Music is a reflection of our soul

Earth Prayer

Place your hands in the soil to feel grounded.
Let the mud ooze through the spaces between your toes.
Wade in the water to feel emotions calm within.
Let the rain shower you and cleanse your spirit.
Fill your lungs with fresh air to blow away those racing thoughts.
Raise your face to the heat of the sun
Close your eyes
Connect with the fire to feel your power.
And look forward to Mother Moon
who will greet you at the end of the day
to tell you she's proud.

Ophelia

The water speaks
Sings into my sadness
To safely drown
Go under and in its caress
Be washed holy
Be cleansed and free
To fill the breaks
I need it
Everyday
To be carried away as if in sleep
He calls me a mermaid
Laughingly says he's never met
Anyone who loves water so deeply
Bath, or rain, or sea
If he only knew
It's the water that loves me

The Eye

The watchful eye
Rises from its slumber
Thanks the moon for looking over its children in the dark
But now it is time
To bring mother to life
To paint the world in vivid color
And feed her flowers and trees
The eye watches
Makes life live
And stays all day
Wants nothing just gives
Gives hope
Gives light
Gives warmth
Until night
When the eye closes
And calls upon the moon
And promises her
She'll come back soon
The clouds mourn
the pastels hold on
Saying good-bye to the eye
Until the dawn

Tree Wonder

Wonder about the life of a tree
What does it see?
The seasons change
It grows
It weathers the storms in hopes to not fall
It houses animals' nests and burrows
I wonder what it would say
When asked about the day
Does it watch the clouds?
Gaze at the stars?
Feel the tiny drops of rain?
Feel the cold snowflakes and
Freeze and crack in the water of hail and ice?
Is it sad in fall as it sheds its colors
The things that brought sunlight into this world?
Does it laugh at the breeze?
Talk to other trees?
I wonder if I could be
As still as a tree
Not searching to see
What's beyond me

Why

Unconditional love,
Hope,
And joy
All wrapped up
In a three-year-old's smile
She's why I do what I do

Times

It's amazing when you think back on the bad times
And your smile bends them into the good times

Put on the lipstick
Kiss the frog
Life's too short
Show up
Be unique
And love
Always love

The Balance Inside

The truth is
we all have
a Jekyll
and
Hyde
A desperation
deep inside
A demon
behind the eyes
A voracious wolf
With a sweet disguise
And the rage comes
and we bear our fangs
A warning set of flash bangs
That creates the tornado
Of hearts and minds
Which way is up?
We chew through
the binds
Eyes full of fears
To the brim with tears
Pleading not to
take away

The one thing that
blocks our way
We don't want to give up
And abandon our love
Only to fight again
Until the calm wind
Blows through
And there
in the aftermath
alone
Is you

All of Us

I pray for those who need strength
I pray for those who need light
I pray for those in waking dark
I pray for those that need to fight
I pray for the good
to shadow over the bad
I pray for the love
to wash away the mad
I pray for the weak
for sometimes they are the strong
I pray for the lesson
that comes when we're wrong
I pray that the universe
hears me today
And listens
and sends positive vibrations their way
We can feel the ones we love
When we are alone
We want to take away their hurt
Their victimized tone
So I close my eyes
and whisper to the wind
And I light a candle
in the name of a friend

I pray the healing will bring a much needed end
And believe in the help this
Small prayer can send
Energy is all there is
And all there will ever be
In all that we can and cannot see
So I start this day
with my intentions clear
And shape my thoughts
for my actions to hear
Our happiness is
in our perspective of what's real
I choose to see with how I feel
I choose hope over dust
I choose faith and choose trust
For this life is much bigger
than all of us

Blessed

I'm blessed to see the crescent moon
before she falls asleep
I'm blessed to watch the sun rise up
from the darkness deep
I'm blessed to care for little ones
that always give a smile
I'm blessed to have some quiet time
even the shortest while
I'm blessed to be inspired
to write my thoughts down every day
I'm blessed to have a loyal man
that loves my witchy way
I'm blessed to have a family
that often cares too much
I'm blessed to have friends
even when I can't keep in touch
I'm blessed and every day
I'm grateful for every breath
For we all know
we'll never know
when the time comes of our death

Confidence

She didn't know her
Beauty
at the time
She didn't know
she'd almost lose her mind
She sauntered across
that high school stage
Inspired some to
turn a new page
That magic moment
when you're someone else
Really just a reflection
of yourself
That siren
with the rhinestone turban
That spider web dress
her mother sewed in
With a fake cigarette
in the holder
She slipped the mink
off her shoulder
A glimpse of danger
In front of strangers
Her confidence was born

Interpretation

It means something to me,
but not to you.
The meaning I said
I thought to be true.
But you said no
and moved to argue.
Maybe I'm wrong.
Maybe you're wrong too.

Moonchild

I wrapped myself in my purple velvet robe
and walked outside in the rain
I unwrapped the shoulders so I could feel
the midnight water on my warm nakedness
I closed my eyes and raised my head up to the sky
One raindrop fell on my lips for me to drink
An offering from the heavens
A cold reminder that I am not alone
The full moon I could not see
For she was inside me

I Am Not a Mom

I'm not a mom
but I know what it's like
To be woken up every two hours
if not every
Thirty minutes to feed crying twin babies
I'm not a mom
but I have worried
when a child has fallen and gotten hurt
I've called 911
called the ambulance
And held the crying child for an hour
waiting for
mom
to come and take over
I may not be a mom
But I have lit the two candles on a child's second birthday cupcake
while mom and dad were out of the country
And when he made a wish
I snapped a picture and made it a Christmas ornament for them to
    always have
I'm not a mom but
I have held a feverish infant for hours
While entertaining her six-year-old sister with short attention span
I am not a mom but
I have woken a child mid-nap to take him to the bathroom
so he doesn't wake up embarrassed about having an accident

I sung endless lullabies while rocking and pacing
just so that baby could sleep
even if it was on me for only ten minutes
I am not a mom but
I have been there
So when you ask, "Are you a mom?"
And I say "No"
only to be met with
"Oh, then you wouldn't understand."
Know that
yes I do
I do understand
For I have been more than just "the help"
I loved and cared
Worried and been scared
for many children
Stayed with them ten hours a day
Fed
Bathed
And taken to school
And picked them up
Taught speech
Reading
American Sign Language
And chased after a deaf two-year-old in a crowded Washington, DC
    playground because he couldn't hear me say, "Wait for me."

I have witnessed first roll overs,
First crawls,
First claps,
First words, and
First steps.
I've inspired children to read
Make art
Play guitar and sing
I am not a mom
But have been a mother to many
I am a teacher.

One thing for sure
I've noticed
the way I've lived my life
these past few weeks
I'm alive
I breathe
I love
Unconditionally
Without reserve
And wildly
Passionately
With friends
Family
And my lover
I have swallowed a few opinions
Banished my judgments
I have just been
Because I allowed myself
to just be
Without fear
Without apology
I give
Without expectation
And kindness can be unexpected
The little things
The smirk
The extra-long hug
The compliments from strangers

The honesty I longed to have
For I can't lie
So promises will be made
In the shadows of the night
Between souls in the bonfire light
In the music of nature as the tree frog sings
In the moonlit feathers that fall from angel wings
The signs are there that I am well on my way
To experience presently the awe of each day
To be thankful and grateful for love and friends
For with each sunrise the moonrise ends
I promise myself and make a vow
That I will live fully in the now
Wherever I shall find it
I will breathe it in and see
That the happiness and love
I've always chased
Is within me

Pure Soul

Gray green eyes like the sea after a storm
Skin that's invitingly soft and warm
Lips as pink as wild petals of the rose
And curves of seduction to the tips of her toes
Words of kindness drip from her lips
Gentle caresses from her fingertips
A soul as pure as the summer rain
A heart that's had its fair share of pain
Ears that have heard the dark demons speak
Hands that hold tightly to the sick and the weak
She stays strong when you are at your worst
It's hard for her to put herself first
Now taking the time to have comfort alone
And dreaming of the day she can call your arms home

Reflection

When you look at the reflection
You don't see what lies beneath
But it is there
Lurking in the depths
The wants
The desires
The motion of the curves
The rhythm of the heart
All you see is light
Mirrored back into your eyes
And what you see
Is perceived through your mind
Which in some times may not be right
I have movement behind my eyes
Thoughts under the skin
The mystery of love remains within
So don't tell me what's there if you cannot see
Close your eyes and it will be clear
Only in darkness can you recover your fear
See with your hands
Feel with your heart
You may not be here
But we are never apart
Once the souls meet
Under the surface of reality
Reflections cease
And love brings peace

Sometimes

Sometimes someone comes into your life
Challenges you, your beliefs, your values, and goals
They do it so easily it can leave you questioning everything you
    believe in
And in the meantime they love you so fiercely
You wonder if you've really known love at all
For you now have feelings you've never experienced before
It's glorious, scary, and exhilarating
So love them back
There are no guarantees
Be grateful you have them
And refuse to let them go
For sometimes you need hidden angels to hold up a mirror to you
    and say
"What the fuck are you doing?
Take my hand. I've never walked this road before, but I don't want
    to do it alone."
You may stumble, and fall, and maybe, eventually, have to finish the
    journey alone.
We all leave this world alone,
but if you don't take the chance how will you ever know if it was
    meant to be?
All you can really offer is hope, love, and faith
Because sometimes you need to take the hand of courage,
encouragement,
and support

to look your future in the eyes and say
"Bring it on—I'm still alive—give me all you got.
This person believes in me.
And I believe I'm in the right place,
right now,
because right now is all I have."
So make the memories
Follow your gut
Screw everyone's opinion of how you should be living…
For we are given one life
One pen
To write our story
Make it good
Make it messy
Make it real
And love hard
Before you run out of ink

Today

Tomorrow will be another today
It will go by fast
And become the past
So live for right now
Anyway you know how
Be grateful and see
That time is not free
Before you know it it's spent
You anticipated it coming
And before you notice it went
And you can't get it back
So don't regret what you lack
Do what your dreams are made of
Have more experiences with what you love
And promise yourself that every day you will strive
For experiences that remind you
You are alive
So snap out of your trance
And give yourself a chance
Let your heart
Teach your soul
How to dance

What I Wish to See

I see the good in everything
I don't have to train my mind
I count my blessings every
Night
no need to remind
I make the best of every minute
For me it's not a task
So the benefit of the doubt is always given
And a second and third chance
And that's not a gift as you may think it to be
Sometimes you have to point out the negativity
I get blinded by the smiles
And the empty promises to change
And leave my heart hoping
It can rearrange
But some people you can't fix
As positive as you may be
The silver lining is full of tricks
A rainbow you may see
But the storm is over
The damage is done
The wreckage everywhere
So see the beauty and hope within
Their weight is too much to bear
Be selfish
You do you

And when it comes to that day
See the goodness in forgiveness
And say what you need to say
For the only person you're one hundred percent
Responsible for is you
Positive
Negative
Helpful
Hurtful
You need to be true
If they lie
Don't cover up
If they try
Help them up
But the good in you
Will never be
A reflection of what you
Wish to see

Alive

I crave
Moments
Laughter
Time I know when I look back
I'll long for it again
Moments when I feel on fire
With people that ignite my spark
I crave the feeling
Of not just being alive
But living

Magic

Magic happens to the believers,
The dreamers,
The go-getters
For they create magic…
Every single day

So glad I picked up the pen
So my truth pours out instead

The thing you're searching for...
Blooms within you

They're Here

Spirits use
Butterflies
As a disguise
Shielding themselves
From my
Eyes
Showing me
Beautifully
That they
Are
Around me

No More Walks through Childhood

No more walks through childhood
The years have all been lived
The carelessness is gone
I have nothing more to give
There were days I'd awake
With not a thing to do
I'd ride my bike down our street
To your driveway to meet you
We'd ride our bikes
In the sun showers
The rays would glisten
Off the droplets of water
That flew all over us
As we sped through the puddles

No more walks through childhood
Of playing hide and seek
Of counting down from
Sixty to one
Trying to resist the urge to peek
This is all that's left of a child's imagination
Ordinary streets with ordinary trees
Where castles and monsters once stood
We've now grown up to see things as they are

This is the aftermath
Of nights spent chasing fireflies
Of walking home from school
Of sledding down the snowy hills in my backyard
And splashing each other in your pool
When the sun shone off your smile
And the wind danced in my hair
Where we hid in the leaf pile
And gave a scarf for the snowman to wear

Us and the rain
And the endless days of wonder
Lasted as long as they could
No more walks through childhood

My heart no longer
Speaks of you

Mad

It's in the grand design
That we must lose our minds
To gain a grateful heart
For only the mad
Truly grasp the pain
And acquire the strength
It takes to move on
And live again

About the Author

Jill Marie Kelly is a Montessori certified pre-school teacher, who has also worked extensively with special needs children and as a certified nursing assistant with severely disabled adults.

She is a musician and artist, who writes to make sense of her world.

CPSIA information can be obtained
at www.ICGtesting.com
Printed in the USA
BVHW030023200219
540658BV00012B/96/P

9 781640 966284